The Snow Queen

ALANA ALBERTSON
Bolero Books, LLC
POWAY, CALIFORNIA

The Snow Queen
A NUTCRACKER Novella
Copyright © 2013 by Alana Albertson

Bolero Books, LLC
11956 Bernardo Plaza Dr. #510
San Diego, CA 92128
www.buybolerobooks.com

Publisher's Note: This is a work of fiction. Names, characters, places, and incidents are a product of the author's imagination. Locales and public names are sometimes used for atmospheric purposes. Any resemblance to actual people, living or dead, or to businesses, companies, events, institutions, or locales is completely coincidental.

Book Layout & Design – JT Formatting
Cover Design by Robin Ludwig Design Inc: gobookcoverdesign.com

Ordering Information:
Quantity sales. Special discounts are available on quantity purchases by corporations, associations, and others. For details, contact the "Special Sales Department" at the address above.

The Snow Queen / Alana Albertson – 1st ed.
ISBN 978-0-9896243-7-4

This book is dedicated to my husband, Roger.
I'd be happy to be trapped in a Winter Wonderland with you.

The flake of snow grew larger and larger;
and at last it was like a young lady,
dressed in the finest white gauze,
made of a million little flakes like stars

-THE SNOW QUEEN by HANS CHRISTIAN ANDERSON

Overture

HE POLICE SWARMED the Strand Theater. Tossing costumes aside, dusting for fingerprints, dousing the floors with Luminol—desperate to find any sign of the Sugar Plum Fairy. Cambridge Ballet's principal dancer, Svetlana Sokolova, had simply vanished—absconded into the night after last night's performance of *The Nutcracker*.

She left nothing behind—except her ballet slippers.

I observed the chaos from stage left. The police had asked everyone who had performed with her to come in for questioning. Since I had played Clara and was on stage for the entire ballet, the police had interviewed me for hours—hoping any little detail that I noticed was significant. The Cambridge Ballet always lured the audience to *The Nutcracker* by casting principals from the company as Sugar Plum Fairy and Cavalier instead of the students from the ballet school like me who danced the other roles. As a member of the pre-professional school, being on stage every night, mesmerized by Svetlana and her Cavalier's *pas de deux* during "Dance of the Sugar Plum Fairy," had been the biggest thrill of my life.

My cheeks felt wet from my tears. What if Svetlana had been kidnapped or murdered? Or a serial killer was on the loose? Was she safe? Would the Cambridge Ballet survive this scandal? I couldn't imagine life without my pointe shoes.

The *Boston Globe's* newest dance critic Mikhail Radetsky approached and handed me a tissue. "Come, now. I'm sure Sveta will be fine."

I dabbed my tears. No way was I going to cry in front of the hottest ballet dancer who had ever graced our stage. While other girls my age obsessed over the cutest member of the latest boy band, Mikhail was the only star of my dreams. "Thank you. I hope you're right. It's an honor to meet you."

Twenty-two year old Mikhail embraced me, and I could feel my heart thump. "Likewise. I couldn't take my eyes off of you last night. Your feet, your musicality, your stage presence enraptured me. You have a big future ahead of you. With your light blue eyes and platinum blonde hair, you will make the perfect Snow Queen."

My eyes widened. Was Boston's most famous dancer complimenting me? It was well known that he was a perfectionist and found fault with almost every dancer in the Cambridge Ballet. "Are you serious? That means so much coming from the best dancer who ever lived! I saw you and Sveta dance Snow King and Queen four years ago. Your partnering made her dancing look so effortless and beautiful."

Mikhail's mouth softened and I saw a glimpse of kindness in his eyes. "You will be a star. How do you say your name?"

"It's Nieves Alba. Nee-A-bays." Though I had a poster of him in a *grand jeté* plastered on my bedroom wall, being in such close proximity with him rattled me. "Mr. Radetsky, I'm so sorry to ask you at a time like this, but would you sign my pointe shoes?" I motioned toward my broken-in, blood-stained Bloch slippers.

Mikhail raised his eyebrows and pulled out a pen to sign the soles. "Please, call me Misha. I want to show you something." He reached into a bag and pulled out a white box. Lifting the lid, he pushed back the crinkly purple tissue paper and removed a beautiful antique snow globe. Inside was a dancer, the Sugar Plum Fairy. Mikhail wound up the globe and she began twirling to "The Dance of the Sugar Plum Fairy."

My fingers trembled as I grasped the globe. The figurine looked lifelike. "It's beautiful. She looks just like Sveta." I shook it and flurries of snow sprinkled on the dancer. I thought for a second that I saw the Sugar Plum Fairy clasp her hands together, ballet mime for begging, but the figure must've not been attached tightly enough.

His eyes shifted. "Funny, I know. Maybe the artist who had sculpted the figurine based it on Sveta's picture. Anytime you want to see it, you can come visit me at my office at the *Globe*." He handed me a business card.

I placed it in my shoes without taking my gaze off the globe. It was breathtaking. The dancer almost seemed alive.

A detective signaled to Mikhail. They were probably glad to have had a reporter on scene last night covering the ballet. Maybe his photographer even captured a clue. "It was nice meeting you, Nieves. I must go. They need me."

He wrapped the globe up in the tissue and placed it back in the box.

"I'd like to follow your career and write an article about your training. Please, stay in touch." Mikhail gave me a kiss on the cheek, his stubble scratching my face, and walked toward the officers.

Evan Stonestreet, who had played the role of Clara's brother Fritz, came from behind me. "What did he want with you?"

"He just wanted to compliment me dancing as Clara. He said I'm destined to be a star. The Snow Queen!"

Evan rolled his eyes. "Lucky you. He hates my guts. Wrote in his review that I had the musicality of a mouse."

"Well, maybe you need to practice more instead of playing video games."

He motioned to the Sugar Plum Fairy's empty costume hanging on a rack, now wrapped in a plastic bag, marked as evidence. "Sveta practiced all the time and now she's missing. And Misha had all the musicality in the world. What did that get him?

3

He tore up his Achilles and ruined his career. Then Sveta left him. Now he's just a critic. He'll never dance again."

"You don't know that. He's doing physical therapy. This critic gig is probably just something to keep him busy. I'm sure he'll stage a comeback." But Evan had a point. Mikhail had dedicated his life to ballet and one bad fall in last year's production of *Giselle* had destroyed his life. Getting injured and being forced to quit dancing was any dancer's biggest fear.

But I didn't want to think about that possibility. I just prayed that Svetlana was safe. I closed my eyes and vowed that one day I would be able to have as perfect of a *passé* as the ballerina had in the globe.

FIVE YEARS LATER

Act I

Scene I

HE HALLS OF Cambridge Ballet were filled with dancers of all ages, crammed around a blank corkboard, silently waiting for the sound of the secretary's footsteps. The list would be up today.

The list.

For as long as I could remember, that list had controlled my life. When I was a little girl, it had been an honor to be given any part in my hometown's production of *The Nutcracker*. My first role had been lamb—and when I had been chosen as the only black lamb, I had felt like a star. Stepping onto the stage for the first time with all the pretty ballerinas made me forget all the yelling that had swirled around me at home.

But for the last five years, the list had been more of a hit list than a cast list. The year after the Sugar Plum Fairy went missing, a Spanish Hot Chocolate had vanished. The next year it was an Arabian Dancer, then the Dew Drop Fairy, and last year a Flower. Despite extensive city and statewide searches, no trace of any of the missing dancers had ever been found, though all their ballet slippers remained behind. Every dancer, director, student, and patron of the ballet had been interviewed, but there were no solid leads. There were theories, though. Plenty of them. The police believed that despite the unfortunate coincidences, none of these cases were related. Maybe a few of the dancers had even left willingly, so they could return later as heroes and be infamous. Svetlana probably ran away to start a new life because it was too painful for her to be around her ex, Mikhail. There had been sightings of the Spanish Hot Chocolate hitchhiking through Montana. The Arabian Dancer had a history of depression; the Dew Drop Fairy was suffering from anorexia. And the Flower had mentioned that she wanted to live off the grid.

But I didn't believe the police. These disappearances had to be related. I knew all of those dancers—trained with them, performed with them, bled with them. Ballerinas that good didn't just throw their years of training out the door to run off and start a new life. Those dancers had all lived in the studio, training up to forty hours a week. I was certain that someone on the new list would vanish, seemingly into thin air, immediately after closing night of *The Nutcracker*.

After the disappearances, the Cambridge Ballet had talked about banning *The Nutcracker*. But the city of Boston begged the artistic director to keep the holiday tradition alive. What was Christmas without *The Nutcracker*? And the Cambridge Ballet simply could not survive without the ticket revenue.

The Boston Police assured the members of the ballet that we were safe. This year, the ballet had installed cameras throughout the theater, and also implemented strict security guidelines. Though many panicked parents pulled their little girls out of the ballet school, there were always more girls waiting in the wings, eager to claim their moment in the limelight.

Mrs. Mosconi opened the creaky door of her office. No one dared crowd her. She gave a smile as she walked toward the bulletin board, holding a single sheet of paper.

It was my year. I was destined to play the Snow Queen; my name even meant snow. Snow Queen was the best role any female dancer in the Trainee program could be cast for. I lived and breathed in the studio and had sacrificed any semblance of a normal eighteen-year-old girl's life to become a ballerina. My non-dancer friends spent their free time sipping frappuccinos, while I was always at the *barre* working on my *frappés*.

Mrs. Mosconi placed the paper up on the corkboard and secured it with a tack. "Congratulations everyone."

Despite the imminent danger, dancers swarmed the board. Cries, screams, shrieks ran through the hall.

I stood back. I couldn't bear to read the list.

Chantal *bourréd* over to me and curtsied. "At your service, my Snow Queen."

I pursed my lips. Mikhail's prediction had come true. I couldn't wait to tell him. All the missing dancers were strong and technically advanced and had lead, solo roles in the ballet. A Snow Queen hadn't disappeared yet—would I be next?

"And I'm your king."

My body tingled hearing Evan's voice. I turned and gave him a hug, breathing in his scent. He was no longer a boy now. A hot nineteen-year-old man stood in front of me—his body seemed to be sculpted by an artist.

I squeezed his arms. "But the Snow Queen has never vanished. I could be next."

Evan blinked and his brown eyes darkened. He pushed his blonde hair off of his face. "Nothing's going to happen this year. You knew Gina—she was always a hippy. I'm sure she left last year just to freak everyone out. She's probably living in Berkeley now."

I wasn't convinced. In my heart I just knew that there was more to the disappearances than the cops knew. Something that couldn't be figured out by detectives. Something—well—creepy.

He clutched me to his chest and kissed my forehead. "Don't worry—I'll protect you."

The only way to ensure my safety was to quit dancing and

drop out of the production. But I would rather risk vanishing without a trace than imagine a life without *pirouetting*.

Act I

Scene II

I TOOK THE Red Line to Mikhail's office at the *Boston Globe*. Ever since we'd met on that fateful night five years ago, we'd developed a rather unorthodox relationship. Though sometimes he would vanish for months and I wouldn't hear from him, he'd always come to my performances. And since I lived thousands of miles away from my family, and all my dance friends were also my competitors, sometimes I felt like Mikhail was the only one who really cared for me.

He motioned for me to come in. "I hear congratulations are in order, Miss Snow Queen."

"Thank you! Are you sure you didn't have anything to do with me getting the role?" My eyes focused on the snow globes on his desk, resisting the urge to wind them up. As a tribute to the missing dancers, he had purchased globes with each of the missing characters inside. He had told me once that seeing them on his desk reminded him to never stop seeking the truth in their disappearances.

"Well, I may have put in a good word for you." His dark hair framed his face, showing off his strong jawline. Mikhail had once been a principal in the Cambridge Ballet, wowing audiences from around the world. Unfortunately, he never had recovered from his injury. Of course, he'd been a suspect in his ex-fiancée's disappearance but his every move the night of that performance had been documented and he was seen leaving the theater with nothing but a briefcase, so he was quickly ruled out.

"It's an honor. I just hope that no one goes missing this year." I looked around the office. It was odd that the walls were bare, without a single photo from his glory days. Maybe it was too painful for him to be reminded of the success he once had.

He took a sip of tea and cleared his throat. "Don't talk of such nonsense. You know I've researched all the cases extensively. It's just a bunch of crazy kids trying to create a scandal—like all of the reality stars who are constantly taking selfies and making pornographic tapes. That last girl, the one who'd played the Flower, she had a history of marijuana use. I wrote a piece on her."

I nodded my head in agreement as my mind raced. Yeah—Gina smoked weed. But I *knew* her. Gina had loved to dance and was looking forward to applying to college. She would've never run off.

"So, Nieves, have you thought about your future? Which companies are you thinking of auditioning for?"

"Well, I always imagined that I would be lucky enough to stay in Boston and dance here. This is my last year of the Trainee Program. I'm hoping they offer me a contract in the Cambridge Ballet II. If not, I'll audition elsewhere."

"Good, that's a solid plan. Many dancers get fooled with talk of attending college. You would waste your best dancing years studying. You can always go back to school after you retire."

My eyes fell back on the globes. What if I snapped my Achilles like he had and could never dance again? If I didn't have an education, how would I support myself? I'd be trapped like the dancers in the globes.

I could feel Mikhail's deep blue eyes watching me. He was twenty-seven now and hotter than ever. I saw him as a sexy ballet star, not the crippled critic who lived in the past. Often I wondered why he'd chosen me as a ballerina to mentor. He was gorgeous—all the girls in the studio lusted after him. Despite my best attempts over the years to flirt with him, he had always shut me down. Once when I was fifteen, I had tried to hold his hand at a coffee shop, but he had withdrawn his hand like a gentleman and gave me a condescending pat on the head. My cheeks had burned with embarrassment. I couldn't believe I had read him wrong. He'd had a hungry look in his eye. I had been sure of it.

I stood up. "I have to go back to practice. I just wanted to stop in and tell you in person."

"I'm so glad you did. I'll be there for every one of your performances. I've been waiting for years to see you perform this role. Seeing you dance always soothes me. You remind me of Sveta when she was your age. When you get a chance—come back and visit. I have an archive of some of the best ballerinas in the world dancing as Snow Queen—Julie Kent, Paloma Herrera, Gelsey Kirkland."

All of my favorite prima ballerinas. To be dancing the same role that they had, and at such a young age, was completely unreal to me. "I'd love that. Actually, Misha, can you do me a favor?"

"Anything. What is it?"

I hesitated. I'd never actually asked him for help, but I needed him. "I was wondering if you could help train me. I'm worried about the *adagio* and I just really want to get it right. I saw you dance the Snow King with Sveta years ago. I know I'm nowhere near as good a dancer as she was, but if you partnered me in practice, I'd dance so much better."

His lips parted. "I'd love to Nieves, but you know I can barely dance with my ankle."

"Maybe you can come by after rehearsal one day and direct Evan and me? He's the Snow King, after all."

Mikhail let out a laugh. "Evan's a decent dancer. But he

doesn't have what it takes to be the best. I hope you see that and don't get involved with him. A boy like that could ruin any chance of you having a great career. What if he doesn't get a contract? Are you going to follow him to some semi-professional ballet company in the middle of nowhere and give up your career? I've seen too many ballerinas with your caliber of talent throw their lives away on young men."

Whoa. Evan and I weren't even dating. He was the notorious ladies man at the studio. Even so, Mikhail was right. Evan and I would be spending so much time together rehearsing. I needed to focus.

I fumbled for my purse. "Okay. Never mind. Forget I asked. I'll just come by another time. Thanks again."

I bundled up into my white winter coat and stepped out of the office into the snow. My blue Hunter boots slushed along the icy road. The sky was dark and the moon glowed in the distance. I should've been scared, a young woman walking alone to the T at night—but the only fear I had was surviving the finale of *The Nutcracker*.

Act I

Scene III

CHANTAL'S LEGS WERE stretched in a wide split. "So who do you think is going to be next? My money is on Clara! You can't have *The Nutcracker* without Clara!"

The younger dancers crowded around Chantal and she laughed.

Little Bella Fortun let out a yelp.

"Stop scaring her," I scolded Chantal. "Bella, don't listen to her. First off, the police and Olivier swear we are safe. They're searching every audience member and there's going to be a metal detector and armed police throughout the theater. Second, everyone who has gone missing has been at least sixteen years old. And finally, Chantal's just mad that she's the Dew Drop Fairy and a Dew Drop has already vanished so she has no excuse to run away."

"Ha. Very funny." Chantal pulled her feet into a butterfly position and pushed down her knees.

I stretched my leg on the *barre* and looked out on the Charles River, watching a crew team row by. Our second floor practice studio was housed in a red brick building. Ever since I'd been accepted to the pre-professional program when I was thirteen, this studio had been my home. I'd left my friends and family behind in San Diego and lived with a host family in Cambridge. The ballet had an arrangement with a local school that allowed me to attend classes around my dance schedule and online. Though I sometimes missed San Diego's weather, I'd fallen in love with Boston's rich culture and historic charm.

Our artistic director, Olivier Beausoleil and the Ballet Mistress, Madame Anna, came from around the corner with a uniformed Boston Police officer.

Great—another useless "you're safe" pep-talk. This would definitely cut into my rehearsal time.

Olivier motioned to the dancers and we all turned and faced the mirrors. "Ladies and Gentlemen. We will be starting rehearsals shortly. Officer Sean Flaherty would like to speak with you regarding safety."

I rolled my eyes. Standard yearly visit from Boston's Finest. We'd all heard the drill before: don't go anywhere alone, be aware of your surroundings, don't let anyone who is not affiliated with the ballet backstage during the productions. Yet despite all these precautions, a dancer still vanished just last year.

Officer Sean nodded his head as if he almost pitied us. He didn't seem like he was there to give a friendly warning. But at least he was sexy. Muscular, dark hair, broad shoulders. He looked very different than the toned male dancers that I'd spent my time with.

"Unfortunately, I have some rather disturbing news. There has been a recent, er, development in the Nutcracker Disappearances. I'm not at liberty to share the new lead, but I urge you all to be extra cautious."

The hair on the nape of my neck pricked my skin. What was he saying—had they discovered a body? I tapped my pointe shoe on the floor, trying to break up my thoughts.

Chantal raised her hand and Officer Sean pointed at her. "Yes, miss?"

She twirled her hair, clearly flirting with him. "So you are just going to endanger all our lives until you decide to share your lead? Maybe you could be my personal bodyguard?"

Olivier glared at Chantal. He always scolded her about her attitude—she was so talented but her lack of solos in the ballet probably had more to do with her mouth than her feet.

Officer Sean's voice deepened. "We will be providing around the clock protection to everyone in the production. All I can say is that there is some evidence that all the disappearances are connected. We have two extra detectives assigned to the ballet school."

I didn't want to listen to the drama. This lecture was cutting into our practice time. Both Evan and Mikhail were watching out for me. I knew I was safe.

A few more dancers asked some questions but Officer Sean didn't give any other information. I zoned out and thought about Mikhail: my own personal dance mentor. Had he never severed his ankle, Mikhail would be the top dancer in the Cambridge Ballet, if not in the United States. The first time I'd seen him dance in *Giselle* with Svetlana, I knew what I'd wanted to do with my life. I wanted to be the best ballerina. I wanted to be her.

The safety brief was over.

I pulled off my knit leg warmers and placed them in my bag. The light on my phone was blinking.

Mikhail: Meet me after practice. At the Peet's in Harvard Square.

My lips stretched into a smile. Maybe Mikhail had reconsidered training me. I texted him back a smiley face and shoved my phone back into my bag before Olivier could see it.

"Let's not let Officer Sean's warnings interfere with the seriousness of our rehearsal. I need my snowflakes and Snow Queen and King." Olivier turned on the music.

Most little girls dreamt of being Clara and of one day dancing Sugar Plum Fairy. I never wanted to be the sweet, sappy Sugar Plum. Snow Queen had always been my goal—dancing in the enchanted forest, welcoming Clara and her Prince into the beautiful winter wonderland on their way to the Land of the Sweets. Tchaikovsky's "Waltz of the Snowflakes" was my favorite piece in the entire score. It was haunting, beautiful, and strangely erotic. And now I would be able to interpret it on my own.

Evan walked over to me, flashing his dimples. "You ready? We've got to kill this, Niev. This is my only shot at getting a contract. I was thinking—" he placed his hands around my waist, as if he was going to spin me, "do you want to get together tonight after and practice?"

I winced. Mikhail's criticism of Evan's dancing rang through my ears. This performance was a crucial showcase for both Evan and me. Our tickets out of the trainee program and into a company. And Evan needed this just as much as I did.

I spun away from him. "I'd love to but I have plans tonight."

"Plans? What could you possibly have to do that is more important than practicing? This is your dream role and you have something better to do?"

I felt like I was betraying Evan. He was my partner, not Mikhail. For me to spend the evening with another man was inexcusable. But I had to convince Mikhail to train me. "I'm sorry. I can't tell you what I'm doing. But I promise it will help our performance."

Evan shook his head, his blonde hair falling into his face. "Is it some guy? I thought you were more serious than that."

Olivier signaled to us to begin our blocking. My stomach fluttered. But I knew that I was doing the right thing. For me. For Evan. For the Cambridge Ballet. For Mikhail.

Act I

Scene IV

RUSHED OVER to the coffee house immediately after rehearsal. My fingers tingled and it wasn't from the ice in my mittens. I wanted Mikhail to look at me as a woman, not as the little girl who had begged him to sign her pointe shoes.

Peet's was packed with the usual coeds, crammed over their books, having lively discussions on literature. I envied their college lifestyle. What would it be like to eat whatever I liked, hook up with guys on the weekend, get wasted and not have to worry about losing the ability to perform the next day? As a dancer, I had to control everything I put into my body. It was a job requirement.

I looked around the coffee house and found Mikhail sitting at a tiny back table, sipping an espresso. He smiled at me, and I walked over to the table.

Mikhail stood from his chair and kissed me on the cheek. I could still imagine him as a graceful dancer. His posture, his chest, his broad shoulders. "Sit, Nieves. I ordered you a latte."

The warm ceramic mug warmed my hands. I took a sip of the sweet coffee. "So Misha, I was—"

"Don't say anything. I want to apologize. You have to understand that as much as I love to, it is painful for me to see you dance. If I had never been injured, I believe you and I would've eventually danced together. I'm not sure I can handle seeing you dance the Snow Queen with another King."

I bit my lip. I knew it was painful for him to watch dancers but I hadn't realized that he felt that way about me. "I'd do anything for you, you know that."

He pulled my hair off my face and turned me around, our faces inches apart. "I will train you. I can teach you everything I taught Sveta. But this must be our secret—I don't want anyone to think I've compromised my journalistic integrity. And I have some rules."

My fingers trembled but his warm hands steadied me. "What kind of rules?"

"The first rule is that you'll stop asking me questions. The second is that you won't tell anyone that I'm training you. The third is you will do whatever I say. The rest you will learn as you go. Come by my apartment after practice tomorrow night and we will begin."

I knew better than to make a secret pact with Mikhail, but I couldn't resist his offer. After all these years, I wondered what it would be like to be in his arms, dancing with him, being his queen.

I kissed him on his cheek. "I can't wait."

His eyes had that hunger in them that I thought I'd seen years ago. Was he attracted to me? I was no longer a girl. He had to know that I was in love with him—begging him to train me. I had opened this door, which I knew he would never cross. Maybe out of fear of rejection or knowing that being close to me could only make the pain of losing his career more acute. Only he could make me into a prima ballerina.

Act I

Scene V

I RUSHED TO class next morning after I overslept. I had been up all night fantasizing about my first training session with Mikhail. What rules did he want me to follow, what had he planned for me? I was prepared to do whatever he asked.

Ballet class was excellent. I felt a renewed energy spew through my body. My *pliés* were deeper, my *tendus* were smoother. Just the thought of dancing with Mikhail had already improved my dancing.

Olivier finished blocking all the choreography for the "Waltz of the Snowflakes." It was technically difficult: *entrée*, *adagio*, two variations and a *coda*. I just hoped I could stay focused enough to give the performance of a lifetime.

Evan waited for me outside rehearsal. "So how was your date?"

I wasn't in the mood to fight with my partner. "Great actually. Since when did you become so interested in my personal life? You've slept with almost every girl in the trainee program."

He smirked and I couldn't help but be intrigued that he cared. Evan was the resident bad boy of our ballet company. He rode a motorcycle, had tattoos, and went out of his way to prove what a badass he was. But I knew that his persona was all an act.

He was just trying to show everyone that he was not an effeminate male dancer. He was the opposite of Mikhail, who always just acted like himself and never felt the need to adopt a hypermasculine image to convince people he wasn't gay. Another reason I'd admired Mikhail.

"I don't care, Niev. But there may be a madman on the loose, and you are my partner, so you're my responsibility. Where were you?"

I didn't want to tell him. Though I knew Evan wouldn't gossip to the other dancers, Mikhail was intensely private. "I was with Misha, okay? He's, uhm, interviewing me for the paper."

Evan's jaw clenched. "You're kidding me? Sure he's just interviewing you. Creepy cripple Misha?"

"Shut up. He's brilliant. And you don't even know him. Why are you such an asshole?"

"Sure, I know him. I've been at this school since I was five. I knew him when he was the star. Always arrogant, never signed autographs. I used to worship the guy. But he treated Sveta like crap. No wonder she left him. It wasn't just because he was injured. He was drunk all the time, cheated on her. I have no respect for him. He probably killed her. You're so naïve."

My neck felt hot. Evan was right—Mikhail had been a jerk back then. But the entire company had treated him like a rock star. He had been young, talented, gorgeous. Why should I blame him for mistakes he made in his past? He was a different man now.

Evan's voice deepened. "Look, do what you want. But you're *my* Snow Queen. We need to pull off the performance of a lifetime in order to get considered for contracts. Let's focus on each other, our *pas de deux*. Trust me, there is something off about Misha."

I walked away from Evan. Mikhail had changed. And I still saw good in him. Everyone deserves a second chance. And I was determined to give him one.

Act I

Scene VI

I BUZZED THE intercom to Mikhail's apartment. The door clicked, and I let myself in. As I walked up the stairs, I could hear my heart beat in my chest. What was I doing here? Mikhail had been known as a playboy in his prime—dates with starlets, affairs with top ballerinas. But he had always been in love with Svetlana. Though the ballet community had crucified her when she had left him after his injury, I had actually understood her. It wasn't just that he could no longer dance. Mikhail had changed. He had started drinking, and there had been rumors of his epic fights with her. She had even quit dancing for a year, trying to coax him into rehab. She finally left him and rejoined the company. In an effort to win her back, he finally went to rehab and got clean. But it was too late—Svetlana had started dating someone else, and Mikhail had lost the two loves of his life.

He opened the door and greeted me with a kiss on my cheek. When I had been younger, I had slept next to this gorgeous man's poster, and now I was at his place.

The scent of strong cabernet wafted in the air, and I heard the sizzling of oil. "Nieves, you look beautiful. I've made dinner." He took off my coat and he glanced at my outfit, a black sweater and tight jeans. "I prefer when ladies dress like ladies.

21

Change into this." He handed me a wine-colored dress and nude high heels, which were in my size.

I had no reason to be modest. Mikhail had seen me in my leotard and tights—he already knew every inch of my body. I pulled the sweater off over my head and wiggled out of my jeans, hoping to get a reaction from him as I stood there in my black lace bra and panties. His eyes explored my body. Was he comparing me to Svetlana? She had a lean, traditional dancer's body—one that I envied. Mine was more curvy, definitely not the ideal for the ballet. He watched me but didn't say a word. I slipped the dress and heels on. "Thank you for making dinner. I can't remember the last time I had a home cooked meal." When I turned eighteen, I had moved into a ballet hostel. Living in the hostel sucked and being a dancer made meal time a chore, not an indulgence. I pretty much survived on yogurt, apples, salads and soups.

"Oh, it's nothing. I don't often have company." Mikhail hobbled back over to the stove. My eyes zeroed in on his hands. I was in way over my head. Dedicating my life to dancing, I'd never had any time to date. Despite a few summer hookups at ballet intensives, I hadn't even been in a real relationship. I was a virgin, but I was determined not to act like one—I wanted to experience Mikhail. Though he could never dance again, the memory of what his body had been able to do on stage filled my head with fantasies of what he'd be able to do to me in bed.

He deglazed the pan and spooned sautéed mushrooms over two petit filet mignons. "I hope you eat steak. The protein will give you power for your performance—and our training."

I smiled and sat at the table. Art hung on the walls, yet as in his office, there were no pictures of him dancing.

He raised a glass of wine. "I know I shouldn't be serving you wine but I wanted to celebrate your role. To my Snow Queen, Nieves Alba. I knew you had it in you the second I saw you dance Clara."

Our glasses clinked and I took a sip. The warm liquid soothed my throat. He placed his hand on my knee and I leaned into him, our lips almost grazing.

I wanted him to kiss me, to feel his hands exploring my body. But he pushed me away from him, and stood up.

"Not yet," he whispered into my ear and handed me a new pair of satin, snow-white pointe shoes, embellished with Swarovski crystals. "I had these custom made for you. Put these on."

"You had these made for me? They're exquisite. Thank you!" As I laced up the slippers, he cleared back the furniture for me. Then he took a black scarf out of his pocket.

"Rule four. You must be blindfolded when you practice. You can't watch yourself dance or see your reflection in the window. True dancing and passion originates within your soul. I've watched you dance, the way you study yourself in the mirror. It's your biggest crutch."

He took the black silk blindfold and tied it around my eyes, so tight it made my eyes throb. How could I dance without seeing my feet? But I trusted him and didn't dare to question him.

"Dance, Nieves. Dance for me."

He turned on his stereo and "The Waltz of the Snowflakes" played over his speakers.

I started my choreography. I heard a creak and I assumed he sat in front of me. I danced for him, courting the music.

"That's it. Chin up, smile. Soften your hands."

Every correction he made challenged me. I went *en pointe* and began my *fouettés en tournant.* One, two, three. I thrust my foot out and in, rhythmically with the music.

"Take your clothes off." His voice sounded breathless.

I slowly slipped the dress off, which fell in a heap by my toes, leaving only my bra and panties behind. I waited to feel his hands around my body but the only sensation I had was the cool air on my skin.

"You're flawless."

"I've never done that many *fouettés*. You bring out the best in me." I glided over the floor. "Dance with me."

"I can't Nieves." I heard his footstep and then his hand clutched my wrist. "You danced beautifully tonight. Take a break." He undid my blindfold and handed me the glass of wine. He pulled me into his arms and I reclined on the sofa.

As I sipped, my head became light. I saw flurries of snow and I must've passed out into a dreamland.

I remembered the smell of nutmeg and chestnuts. The missing dancers were there, performing their final roles in a breathtaking winter wonderland. I tried to talk to them, ask where they had all been hiding, but they all just gave me a frozen stare.

Except Svetlana.

When she saw me, she held her hands in front with her palms out and turned away from me—ballet mime for fear.

Mikhail ignored her and took my hand. His foot showed no sign of the injury that had destroyed his career. When the "Waltz of the Snowflakes" played, Mikhail and I danced together as Snow King and Queen. My steps were perfect and he was dancing better than he ever had.

He partnered me in the *pas de deux* and I executed all the steps with ease. His touch was gentle and kind, yet at times possessive and forceful. He placed his strong hands on my thighs, then glided them up to my waist. I had never danced so many flawless *pirouettes*, with his hold guiding me.

But it was only a dream. I awoke the next morning on his sofa.

"Nieves, thank God you are okay. I knew I shouldn't have given you wine when you probably don't have a tolerance. You passed out." He poured me a cup of coffee.

I took a sip of the coffee, my head pounding. "I had the craziest dream. We were dancing together. Snow King and Queen. And all the missing dancers were there also."

He laughed. "Wouldn't that be wonderful? I would give anything to dance again—especially with you as my partner. But those days are long gone and I doubt I will ever dance again without a miracle. Come, you must get ready for class. We can try rehearsing again tomorrow."

I finished my coffee and gathered my coat, rushing to leave. What a fool I had made of myself! Squandering the opportunity of a lifetime to get free training from one of the top dancers. Instead, I had passed out like a lightweight. Mikhail must've thought I was so immature.

Mikhail walked me out of his house and hailed a taxi. When it arrived, he gave me a kiss on the lips. I stuffed myself into the cab, trying to replay last night in my mind. The arch of my foot was throbbing, as if I had danced all night. But I hadn't been *en pointe* for more than fifteen minutes. The only other dancing I had done yesterday besides morning class was in rehearsal and we had only marked the choreography.

Reaching into my bag, I grabbed my tape and wrapped my ankle. Something caught my eye—the sole of my right pointe shoe seemed lumpy. My fingers traced the sole and I discovered a tiny piece of paper was tucked into the lining of my pointe shoe. I pulled it out and read it—"Help us!"

Who had written that? Mikhail had only given me the slippers last night. Maybe Mikhail's personal cobbler had a wicked sense of humor?

I put the paper in my wallet. The cab pulled up in front of the studio. Reporters congregated outside, and cameramen were setting up their equipment.

I walked over to Evan, who was standing next to Chantal. "What's going on?"

Evan took a drag on a cigarette, which was super odd, since I'd never seen him smoke. "They found Svetlana's body. She was washed up on the banks of the Charles River—wearing her pointe shoes."

My bag hit the icy ground with a thud. I had just seen her in my dreams and she had seemed so real. Was it one of those supernatural visits from the dead? Maybe she was a ghost and trying to tell me something about her killer? I didn't believe in all that nonsense but I couldn't explain that I felt like she was trying to warn me about something. Probably not to perform in the ballet.

Maybe *The Nutcracker* was cursed. Ever since I'd been cast, my world had shifted. I was destined to be Snow Queen and nothing was going to stop me from dancing in *The Nutcracker* on Christmas Eve.

Intermission

A WEEK HAD passed since they discovered Svetlana's body. The tabloids had a field day with the news: "The Death of the Sugar Plum Fairy," "Corpse de Ballet", and "There's a Nut(cracker) on the Loose." An autopsy had been performed and it was determined that she had drowned, and the toxicology report came back clean. What was truly baffling was that despite her being missing for the past five years, the coroner determined that she had only been dead for less than four hours when her body was found.

Where had Svetlana been for the past five years? Had she been hiding out somewhere in Boston? It made absolutely no sense. Everyone had been looking for her: the police, the public, I mean hell—she'd even been featured on *Nancy Grace*. If Svetlana had been in New England for the last five years, someone somewhere would have noticed her.

I'd had many late night rehearsals at the ballet and hadn't seen Mikhail since that night. Especially since the police were stalking his every move because he had once been engaged to Svetlana. I had to give a sworn statement that I was with him the entire night before her body was discovered, which was the God's honest truth. Thank God I had been with him or he wouldn't have had an alibi. I'd been in his arms all night—though I definitely didn't mention that I'd passed out in his place. Nor a word about my crazy dream that Svetlana was in. I didn't want the police to think I was some nut job.

But I needed to see him. He hadn't returned any of my texts

or phone calls. I was sure he was just distraught about Svetlana.

Snow covered the ground. Svetlana's discovery had put a damper on Cambridge's Christmas spirit. Though garlands, mistletoe, and ornaments were all threaded around Harvard Square, the lights decorating the trees all seemed a little less bright than they had in the past years. The faint smell of ginger from the two gingerbread lattes I carried even did little to ease the rumbling in my stomach.

I buzzed Mikhail's door. When he didn't answer me, I began pounding on the window.

"Misha, please, let me in."

The door opened. Mikhail didn't say a word. He had no shirt on and was wearing pajama bottoms. Sporting a full beard, he looked more like a Navy SEAL than a former ballet dancer—which I found irresistible.

The room reeked like vodka and cigarettes. Heat radiated from the old school furnaces.

I handed him a latte. "This wasn't your fault."

"Of course it was my fault. Once I tore my ankle up, I went crazy. I was horrible to Sveta. I drank, cheated. Blamed her for my injury because she convinced me to dance as Dracula. I never wanted to take the role. I drove her away and then she vanished. And now she's dead."

I placed my latte on the entry table and hugged him. "No one blames you. You were depressed. You'd lost your identity. But you've reinvented yourself. I wish Sveta could see what you became. She'd be proud of you."

He turned away from me. "Nieves, leave. You shouldn't be here. I'll just destroy you. I don't ever want to hurt you. You're the only woman I've ever met that has been interested in me for who I am, not for what I can do for you. Once I lost my talent, everyone abandoned me. But not you. I'm no good for you."

My heart broke hearing about his pain and guilt. I'd never imagined how lonely he must've been. I took his hand. "I love you, Misha."

He pulled me onto the chair. I straddled him, pressing my hips down on his lap. The years of longing were about to come to an end.

His eyes lit up and I saw intensity in them that I had only seen in old videos of him dancing. "I'm not who you think I am. The dancer you fell in love with when you were a little girl died years ago."

If that was his attempt at dissuading me it was having the opposite effect. I didn't pity him like he might've thought. I worshipped him, for reinventing his life and becoming a dance critic. For moving on after Svetlana left him and then disappeared. But most of all, for believing that I could become a prima ballerina before I had believed in it myself.

I took his face in my hands and kissed his lips. He came alive underneath me. His hands caressed me while his tongue explored my mouth. His warm, moist kisses ignited a fire in my body. This beautiful man had been the object of my fantasies for years.

His blue gaze pierced through me. "You're too good for me. I will destroy you."

"I've wanted you since the day you signed my slippers. Even before then. I won't abandon you, Misha. I'm not like her."

Apparently those words did the trick. Mikhail scooped me up and laid me in front of the fireplace. I expected him to ravish me, but instead he savored every touch, every kiss. I'm sure he could sense that it was my first time, and that I'd been waiting to be with him for years. I wasn't in any hurry.

He pulled off my top, and slowly explored my body with his hands. His years of training had given him a lean but muscular body and I marveled at his strength. He hovered on top of my body, supported by his arm and I felt like we were dancing in Mozart's Petite Mort. My body writhed under his, completely wet with anticipation.

He undressed me, pausing to study the curves of my body. I tried to dominate him, to take some semblance of control, but he would just smile and flip me back over and have his way with me—not that I was complaining. He licked my neck, my breasts, and my nipples, as his fingers traced down my thighs. I let out a moan when the tips of his fingers penetrated me, dancing in between my panties and my warmth.

Just when I thought I was going to scream in pleasure, he stopped. "This isn't right. You are too young. You should date someone your own age, like Evan." He studied my eyes.

My lips quivered. "I don't want Evan—he's just a boy. I want you. Only you. I've never been with anyone—I want you to be my first, and only."

His jaw dropped and his mouth widened into a smile. He kissed me softly on the lips. "I love you too, Nieves. My Snow Queen. But you must promise never to leave me. I couldn't bear ever losing you. Watching you dance over these last years, following your career, living through your steps, has been the only thing that has kept me going. If we commit to each other and you vanish, I could never go on."

My pulse raced. "I promise."

My words elicited a frenzied response from him. He took my panties off and dove in between my legs, licking, sucking, teasing me.

"Misha, I—" My breath shortened, my heart pounded. I'd never experienced anything close to this pleasure. Throbbing, fluttering, melting from his touch, his tongue, his mouth.

"Come for me, Nieves."

Pleasure exploded through my body. Once, twice. I screamed for him. No one had ever made me feel like he had. No one had ever made me dance like he had. I was addicted.

I collapsed on the rug. He pulled me to him, and I curled up in his arms.

Though I was satisfied, I wanted more. I wanted to give him

pleasure, take away his pain. I wanted to feel him inside me. If our bodies couldn't become one on the stage, then at least we could dance together in the bedroom. "I want to please you. Teach me how."

He stroked my hair. "Not tonight, babe. I want you to save your energy for opening night. After closing night, you will truly be mine."

What a selfless man. He truly adored me and wanted nothing but to pleasure me and nurture me in return. How had I lucked out?

I cuddled up next to him and we fell asleep.

We woke the next morning, our bodies still entwined. But like the last time I spent the night at his house, I'd slept restlessly. And the nightmare had returned.

This time, I was in a small cottage, with a wood-burning fireplace. Snow covered the ground outside and I was sobbing. The walls were bare and I didn't have a telephone, a television or a computer. But my Snow Queen costume was hanging on the door.

I rolled out of bed, careful not to wake sleeping Mikhail. The radiant heated floor warmed my feet and I tiptoed into the bathroom. I touched the back of my neck, and felt a drop of blood, which wasn't shocking because Mikhail and I couldn't keep our hands off each other last night. I slid into the shower, and turned on the hot water.

Was I his girlfriend now? How would our relationship affect my career? Surely with his influence and guidance I would now get a contract in the Cambridge Ballet.

As I lathered up my body, I thought I heard Mikhail wake. Maybe he'd jump in with me. I rinsed the suds off and heard footsteps.

"Morning, love." Mikhail opened the shower door and embraced me.

He began kissing my breasts and licking my stomach. The

steam from the shower fogged up the glass. I couldn't wait until closing night—I wanted to feel him inside of me right then. But when the steam faded, I could see my neck in the reflection of the mirror. The words, "Help Us" had been etched into my neck.

I pushed Mikhail off me and covered my neck with my hand.

"What's wrong?"

"Oh nothing, my throat hurts. That's all. I just hope I'm not getting sick." I opened the shower door.

He followed me out. "I'll make you some tea."

When he turned the corner, I quickly got dressed and wrapped my scarf around my throat. Those scratches hadn't been there last night. Who was asking for help? Was this connected to the Nutcracker disappearances? Or Svetlana's murder? Was Mikhail involved?

Mikhail appeared with a cup of tea. "Nieves, you've made me happier than I thought was possible. When I was a star, everyone always wanted something from me. But I know you love me for who I am and you don't care that my body is lame." He paused and I leaned into him. "After the finale, will you go away with me?"

"I'd go anywhere with you."

Maybe my mind was playing tricks on me. But I couldn't shake the feeling that Mikhail held the key to the mystery of the Nutcracker disappearances and I was close to figuring out for certain what had been haunting America's beloved ballet.

I knew what I was doing with Mikhail was right. My relationship with him had changed, and now for the first time since I could remember, I saw a world beyond the stage lights and the *barre*. I wanted to make a life with Mikhail. And I was prepared to sacrifice anything to be with him.

I covered up the back of my neck with the collar of my jacket. I had to get to the studio—I had the performance of a lifetime to focus on.

Act II

Scene I

HE THEATER WAS surrounded by Boston's Finest, FBI and a SWAT team. Every local and national news affiliate had reporters and cameramen camped outside. It was closing night of *The Nutcracker*. And now that Svetlana's body had been found and the disappearances had been upgraded to possible homicides, no one was taking any chances on another dancer vanishing.

The two-week run of *The Nutcracker* had been a brilliant success. I'd danced better than I ever had, thanks to Mikhail's private coaching.

He'd come to every performance and sat in his private box seat. I was so lucky that he was so supportive. Everyone in the company suspected that we were an item. All the dancers were really supportive—except Evan. His eyes shot icicles at me when he found out. But he didn't say a word. However, our dancing had suffered. He partnered me more aggressively, less passionately, less lovingly. I tried to talk to him about it and he just said, "Don't worry about it. You're just making a mistake." I didn't understand his jealousy at all. We'd never dated, nor had we ever hooked up. He'd never shown any interest in me at all. So what was his problem?

I didn't have time to figure it out. I'd pushed the feelings that I was in danger out of my head. Tonight was the last night that I would ever dance Snow Queen for the Cambridge Ballet. And immediately after, I was going away with Mikhail. I couldn't wait.

The Boston Symphony Orchestra began to play Tchaikovsky's famous score. The first notes gave me chills. My blonde hair was pulled into a tight bun and silver glimmer shadow enhanced my ice blue eyes. I laced up my special pointe shoes and stretched behind the curtains.

Evan walked over to me, dressed in his shiny tunic. I had to admit, he looked gorgeous. I was overcome with emotion. This could be our last time dancing together. We'd been put together as partners since we were kids. What if we didn't get contracts at the same company?

I peeked out the curtains. The party scene was in full effect. I marveled at the colorful costumes, the decorated Christmas tree, the shiny gifts. Evan pulled me behind the scaffolding. "Nieves, listen to me. I want you to be careful tonight. I can't help but think that you're going to vanish."

"Well I'm not going to vanish. You don't need to worry about me." I paused—Mikhail had sworn me to secrecy about our upcoming trip, and I hadn't told a soul. But something in the back of my head wanted to tell someone. Just so no one would think that I was another casualty of *The Nutcracker* curse. I lowered my voice. "Misha and I are going to go away together tonight. Just for a few days. Don't tell anyone."

His hand clenched, then he ran it through his hair. "Are you kidding me? You can't go anywhere after the show. Everyone will think you were kidnapped. We all have strict orders to report back to the stage immediately after the curtain closes. Misha knows this. Why on earth would you possibly think this is a good time to go on a romantic rendezvous?"

Evan had a point. But I'd already made a promise to Mikhail. It's not like I wasn't going to come back. "Relax. It's just for a few days. We just wanted some time alone together. I'll be fine."

The Mouse King was fighting the Nutcracker. "Waltz of the Snowflakes" was coming up next. I rubbed my shoes in the chalk and prepared to take the stage with the snowflakes.

It was showtime.

My snowflakes *bourréd* onto the stage, hiding me in their circle. When they opened and presented me, the audience roared. My face lit up and I began to dance. Knowing that Mikhail was watching me in the audience excited me. My arms were artistic, my *passé* was precise, my turns were tight. I didn't miss a beat. When Evan came onstage to join me, I knew we were going to have our best performance yet.

Evan's leaps weren't as high as Mikhail's once were, nor was Evan as strong as Mikhail had been in his day. But Evan danced with an intoxicating blend of exuberance, passion, and playfulness. He was a strong partner, knowing when to gently guide me and where to relinquish control over me.

We danced our *pas de deux* and the crowd went wild. Cheers and claps filled the auditorium. I was so caught up in the moment, that after the curtain closed, I jumped and kissed Evan.

He kissed me back, soft, sweet, tender. "Nieves. Please. Don't go with Mikhail."

It was too late. Mikhail was standing backstage. Waiting for me, holding a dozen white roses.

I gave Evan a hug and he held me tight, his hand resting on the back of my tutu. Turning away, I walked toward Mikhail and took his hand and waved off the security guard.

I couldn't wait to be alone with Mikhail.

Act II

Scene II

IKHAIL LED ME to a secret room under the stage. It was filled with roses, articles he had written, and pictures of him dancing. "Wow—I never knew this room existed."

He was dressed in a handsome Tom Ford suit. He had cleaned up so nicely since I'd seen him that night at his apartment. He was clean-shaven and smelled of fresh cut pine. Yum.

"It was actually a dressing room once before the renovations. Sveta and I discovered it one night and it became our secret hideout." He took out a bottle of wine from his briefcase, and a small box. "Congratulations, Nieves. You were perfect. Here—this is for you."

He poured me a glass of wine as I opened my present. Though I was pretty sure that I knew exactly what he was about to give me. I unwrapped the paper and saw a reflection. Yes. A snow globe. After all these years, he'd finally bought me my own.

"I knew how much you admired the one I had. This one is actually custom made for you. You were right, the ballerina in the other globe looked too much like Sveta so I got rid of it."

I took the globe out of the box, but there was no dancer inside of it. My face dropped. Who wanted a nutcracker snow globe with no ballerina inside?

But I didn't want to hurt his feelings. "Thank you. It's beautiful." I kissed him and ran my hands on the back of his neck.

He pulled back from me and I took a sip of the wine, a chardonnay. It was crisp and had hints of vanilla, apples and oaks. I swirled the glass and kept sipping. I didn't want to get drunk and pass out again, especially since we were going to leave on our trip. But what was the harm in having just one drink. After all these weeks of rehearsals, and the stress of the discovery of Svetlana's body, I needed to relax.

Mikhail watched me intently. He turned me around and started rubbing my shoulders as I sipped the wine. His hands dug into my knots, alleviating the tension in my shoulders, neck and back. The room felt warm and I became woozy. I took one last sip and relaxed into Mikhail's arms.

He stroked my forehead. "You can take a quick nap if you like. You must be exhausted after dancing tonight. I'll wake you in a bit and we can set off for our getaway."

I nodded my head but I was too weak to speak. Mikhail rubbed my temples. What a perfect night. I'd danced my heart out, my boyfriend was so romantic, and we were about to officially start our relationship together. I closed my eyes and Mikhail kissed me on the lips.

Act II

Scene III

HE WARMTH FROM the fire covered my body and the scent of nutmeg tickled my nostrils. My eyes opened, and took in my surroundings. It seemed I was in a cozy cottage, like the one that I had dreamt about. I was lying by the fire, Mikhail humming in the background, while snow blitzed the window.

"Good morning, sleepy head." His eyes twinkled and he walked toward me. Without his limp.

"Good morning? What happened last night? Last I remember, I had some wine. Where are we? And oh my God! Misha—you aren't limping at all?"

His toes straightened and he went on to demi-pointe.

My mouth dropped. Had he healed overnight? Was watching me perform truly some kind of mystical salve for his ankle? What in the hell was going on?

He lowered his feet down into fifth position, pointed his right toe to the side and then into fourth position. Then lifted his right toe into *passé* and executed the ten most perfect *pirouettes* I had ever seen.

"Misha, you're cured! How did this happen?"

He lifted me over his head. "Yes. Thanks to your love and strength. I didn't want to tell you because I didn't want to get your hopes up. But I've been going to this experimental physical therapy for months. I thought there was no hope. But we had a breakthrough the other week and I can dance! I've been limping on it purposely as to not spoil the surprise for you. But I'm cured."

He placed me down and gave me a deep kiss. Never in my wildest dreams could I have imagined that we would one day be able to dance together. Before I said a word, he pointed to my slippers, which I quickly put on. He turned on his iPod and played "The Waltz of the Snowflakes."

His arms wrapped around me and we glided into the snow *pas de deux*. He was a much better dancer than Evan was, though it was hardly fair to compare them. Mikhail's feet were fast and elegant, and his toes seemed to skate across the floor. When he lifted me into angel lift, I felt like I was flying. His hands knew where to touch me, where to support me and where to turn me. It was as if I was born to dance with this man.

He set me down on the floor. I jumped into his arms and he caught me.

"Misha. Oh my God! That was amazing. I've always wondered what it would be like to truly dance with you, be your partner. You can go back to the Cambridge Ballet. We can start a new life together. It's a miracle."

Mikhail didn't say a word, but I could read his eyes. It was time. He wanted me.

He turned his iPod on to the Arabian Dance from *The Nutcracker*. I knew the piece, having danced it two years ago. I danced around the fire for him, teasing him and taunting him. He sat down on a sheepskin rug, seeming to enjoy the view. I slowly peeled my clothes off my body. I seductively moved my body, my hips, my breasts. The hypnotic music mesmerized him.

I lay down on the floor. He climbed on top of me, yet he was still dancing. We played with the music and the beat, until I couldn't resist him another minute. I wanted to become one with him, experience true unity through dance and love.

Our naked bodies writhed together, and he entered me. I gasped—it was my first time and the pain masked the pleasure. He tried to be gentle, but I could feel his years of longing coming alive inside of me. I breathed in, trying to endure for him, hoping the throbbing would dissipate.

"Nieves, are you okay?"

I clenched my teeth. "Yes."

The thrusting, pulsating, became more intense. This was what I'd been waiting for, dreaming of for all these years. I was a dancer; I was used to the intersection of pain and pleasure.

He finished and collapsed on top of me. Tears welled in my eyes. I didn't want to cry but I couldn't control myself.

"Babe, I'm so sorry I've caused you pain. It will get better. I'll teach you how to please me."

I rolled over, embarrassed that I was crying. He'd been with the most beautiful women, and he probably saw me as some pathetic virgin.

He kissed my tears. "I'm gonna run to the store and get us lunch. Please, take these to help you relax. I'll be back before you know it." He handed me two small blue pills.

I clutched them in my hand. Was he trying to drug me? He didn't want to cuddle with me? He'd been so tender the other night. Something seemed off. "I will take them after I bathe. Where are we by the way? You never told me."

He got dressed and looked toward the door. "Upstate New York. In my friend's cabin. I'll be back soon." He grabbed his coat and slammed the door shut.

I broke down in tears. This wasn't how I wanted it to happen. I thought he would please me first, like he had done the other night. But I guess no one's first time is a fairy tale.

I stepped into the shower, and warm water washed away the blood that had trickled down my legs. Mikhail could dance again. We had our whole future together. But I couldn't shake a

41

sinking feeling. Why did I feel so alone?

I stepped out of the shower, and heard a strong rap at the door. Was Mikhail back already? Didn't he have a key?

Squeezing the water out of my hair, I wrapped myself in a white terry robe that was hanging on the door.

The knocking became louder. What was his problem?

I walked to the door and opened it. But it wasn't Mikhail.

Evan stood in front of me, his clothes drenched from snow.

"What are you doing here, Evan? Did you follow me? What's wrong with you?"

He pushed himself into the door. "Fuck yeah, I followed you. Mikhail left you here alone. You're not on some romantic getaway as he promised. He's trapped you in a snow globe!"

The snow globe?! "Are you insane? We're in upstate New York."

He pulled me outside, the icy snow freezing my feet. "Look up, Nieves. Does upstate New York have a glass ceiling? Do you hear 'The Waltz of the Snowflakes?'"

My eyes opened and I could see that shiny roundness of a dome above my head. I closed my eyes and heard the faint sound of "The Waltz of the Snowflakes" playing.

There had to be an explanation. My lip quivered.

Evan shook me. "Wake up, Nieves! He's responsible for the disappearances. He killed Sveta. Haven't you noticed anything strange?"

I thought back to the perfect row of snow globes on his desk, how each one looked like one of the missing dancers.

How had I been so blind? Svetlana, the dreams! And of course he could dance perfectly in here. Was I trapped forever? He'd been kidnapping all the dancers?

"How did he trap me in here? And how did you get in here?"

Evan pushed me back in the house and took off his clothes, throwing them near the fire. His naked body glistened. I couldn't help but stare. "I drank the wine he gave you. We don't have much time. The other dancers are waiting to escape. They told me that the window to the globe only opens when he winds it up from the day *The Nutcracker* cast is announced until Christmas Day. They've been trying to flee for years. Sveta tried last month but he caught her and killed her. At midnight tonight, the globe will close until next year. According to the girls, Mikhail will visit you one last time in a few hours. You have to get ready."

Evan stormed into the bedroom and put on some of Mikhail's clothes. I didn't have time to question him, or think about how ridiculous this sounded. But in my heart, I knew Evan spoke the truth. I'd been deceived. Mikhail didn't love me—he had used me. Harnessing my dance skills in the globe so he could feel whole again. What was he? A man, a demon, the devil? I didn't know or care. I just needed to make sure I escaped this globe.

Act II

Scene IV

GINA, CALLIE, KELSEY, and Sharon huddled together in the shack near the globe exit. They'd filled me in on how Mikhail had seduced each and every one of them—promising them free lessons, fame, and love. Apparently after that dream that I'd had where I'd seen them, Svetlana had enough and tried to escape, hoping to alert and save me before it was too late. She'd run to the exit but Mikhail had caught her and thrown her out of the globe. No one was certain how she had ended up in the Charles River, though they suspect that while I was passed out on his sofa, Mikhail had taken her and thrown her in the river.

I was chilled thinking that she'd ended up dead because of me.

The plan was for them to hide by the entrance and I would stay in the cottage, waiting for Mikhail. Evan would lie in wait with me, and try to trap Mikhail so we could escape. The girls knew that they were risking their lives trying to escape, but they wanted to try. I begged Evan to leave with the girls, but he wouldn't consider it.

Night fell and the globe lit up. It was very beautiful, lit up with the Christmas lights. The girls had told me that it wasn't all bad in here. They could visit other neighboring snow globes.

There was an abundance of food, and drinks. The snow globe city council was very supportive of the arts and neighbors from surrounding globes all came out to support the ballerinas. Still—they all missed their freedom.

Evan and I sat in the cottage. The silence was deafening. "Evan, I'm so sorry I didn't listen to you and I dragged you into this."

"It's okay, Nieves. You didn't know. I get it. Let's just try to focus on getting out of here."

How had I been so stupid to never appreciate this great guy who had always been by my side? Sure, he'd dated all the girls in the company, but straight male ballet dancers were always trying to prove to the world how masculine they were.

The vibration of footsteps shook our globe. Evan nodded at me, and went to hide in the closet.

Mikhail opened the door, carrying a dozen roses, coffee, and a bag of sweets. "Nieves, my love, you look scared. Are you okay?"

My blood burned. "I'm fine. Where were you?"

He placed the goodies on the table. "Just shopping for my Snow Queen."

He approached me for a kiss but I recoiled. I was a dancer, not an actress.

His eyes narrowed. "What's wrong?"

I knew my script, what I needed to say to Mikhail. But I didn't know if I had the strength to stand up to him. "Nothing, I just missed you." I let him kiss me, but his smell revolted me. I couldn't hold back, knowing that my words would risk any chance our plan had of succeeding. "I know about Sveta. And the others. What are you? A demon? What about everything you ever said to me? Was it all a lie?"

No impulse control. I'd just blown my cover and I knew I'd have to pay.

Mikhail's hand clenched, and a vein bulged in his neck.

46

"Ha, little girl. I've been in love with your dancing since I met you. The perfect addition to my arsenal. I'm not capable of love. The only woman I ever loved was Sveta, and she betrayed me. This is now the only place I can dance, and become alive. But don't worry, I'll treat you well in here, providing you behave."

Evan burst out of the closet, yielding a sword we'd found from a Mouse King costume. "Don't touch her, Misha. You sick fuck. I always knew you were behind the disappearances. All of the girls were in love with you but I saw through you. You can dance in here but in the real world, you are nothing but a has-been."

He looked sharply at Evan, then me. "Sorry Nieves, I thought you were different and that you would be happy in here."

I thought Mikhail would rush toward Evan, try to fight him. But Mikhail until the end was a coward. Evan lunged toward Mikhail, and Mikhail bolted out the door. He *grand jeté'd* toward the opening in the globe. Evan and I bolted after him, but our leaps were no contest for Mikhail. He'd been a danseur, and we were still in Cambridge Ballet II.

The "Waltz of the Snowflakes" was ending. And when the song ended, so did our chance to escape.

We watched as Mikhail leapt through the globe. My heart broke as the opening began to close. I started to execute one more leap, but Evan took my hand and held me back. "There's no point, Nieves. It's closed. We're stuck here."

At least the girls had escaped and were hopefully reuniting with their families.

I wrapped myself up in Evan's arms. "I'm so sorry. You must hate me."

He pushed my chin up with his thumb. "No, I could never hate you. I've loved you since I first saw you attempt an arabesque when you were nine. And the way you yelled at Madame Anna for telling Chantal that she was fat. You fight for what you believe in. You were so different than the other girls. When they were distracted with clothes, shoes, new cars, you were always focused on your dancing." He tilted his head and kissed me.

The globe sprinkled snow around us. His warm, soft lips had a tenderness that Mikhail's lacked. I wiped the tears from my eyes. We'd just lost our freedom, but we'd found each other.

Apotheosis

THE SNOW PELTED down from the top of the globe, reminding me that I would be trapped forever.

But I didn't mind.

We'd settled into our new life quite nicely. Being trapped in a snow globe wasn't that bad. Evan and I still danced, and inside the globe we never made mistakes. We had free health care, food, and housing. Our little bungalow was small but cozy. I'd gone to the local craft globe and decorated our home with pictures of the world outside the globe to remind me of home. We'd even made friends with people in neighboring globes.

I finally understood why Mikhail wanted to live in here with me. Everything was perfect. No crime, no poverty. Just a picture-perfect year round winter wonderland.

Had Mikhail explained it to me, I might have considered living here with him. But I just felt so trapped and abandoned. And he didn't want to reside here full time with me. He wanted to visit me on his terms and still maintain his freedom in Boston, like he had with Sveta. I deserved more than that life. More than he could give me.

Evan stoked the fire. His bare chest glowed against the backdrop of the flames. He wore long dark pajama bottoms that hung over his perfect body. I was so lucky he had decided to stay with me. And I was so happy that the other girls had been able to escape. Their freedom was worth my sacrifice.

"What did you want to do today, babe? I was thinking we

could go sledding with the dogs?" He pointed to our two American Eskimo dogs that we had recently adopted from a neighboring globe, both asleep by the fire.

"Sure, sounds great." I stood up and kissed him on the lips. He melted back into me. This was love. Not that fucked up idol worship relationship I had with Mikhail. How had I not seen that he had groomed me since I was a little girl? Evan had always been there for me. We grew up together, trained together, and now we would be together forever. I just wished I had let myself fall for him sooner. But he forgave me for being with Mikhail. And I had forgiven him for hooking up with every girl in our company, trying to make me jealous. But we were both just finding ourselves. I mean how many people meet their soul mates when they are nine years old?

Evan scooped me up and carried me to the bedroom. He covered my body in kisses.

I gasped in delight. "I'd rather spend a lifetime with you trapped in this globe, than be free in Boston. You are my home. I love you, Evan." I stared down at the small diamond ring on my left hand. He had proposed to me on New Year's Eve. We planned a small wedding and he was trying to rent out a sand globe from Hawaii for our honeymoon.

He kissed my neck. "Love you, too." I couldn't be certain—but I swear the light snowfall turned into a blizzard. Dammit—Mikhail must be shaking the globe again.

Tears welled in my eyes. This was all my fault. Guilt swept across my face. "We're stuck here forever. Unless he lets someone else in the globe and we can escape."

Evan let out a laugh. "Don't worry about it, Nieves. I'm happy here. No auditions, no stressing about contracts. Just you and me. The girls are probably trying to scheme a way to save us—since no one would believe them if they told the truth. And one day, he'll slip up and we'll be able to leave. I'll be ready for next year's *Nutcracker*." He turned on his iPod and blasted some heavy metal to drown out that damn "Waltz of the Snowflakes" song. Pulling off my slip, he looked like he was going to devour me. "Let's give him something to watch!"

I giggled and he threw me down and we made love.

Even sex was better in the globe.

Encore

THE BLIZZARD BLANKETED the small Ukrainian town in a sheet of snow. Mothers huddled with their children under warm coats, as they scurried home before the roads were closed.

Inna Danilova didn't mind the cold. She loved the pristine beauty of the snow. So pure, so untouched, so innocent.

She slugged her pointe shoes in a bag over her shoulders. The shoes were old, her sister's. But her family couldn't afford new ones and Inna was grateful to have the pair. She had only been on pointe for the last year, but since she had just been cast as Masha, the role Americans called Clara, in *The Nutcracker*, she was eager to focus on her training.

The old, decrepit ballet theater had recently been renovated by a mysterious handsome man. He spoke perfect Ukrainian, and rumors had it that he had once been a ballet star back in the United States. He walked with an affected gait, and Inna assumed he had been injured dancing. She didn't dare ask him about what had happened—everyone in the town was just so thrilled that this wealthy man had brought the arts back into their town. Classes were free and this year they were going to stage the town's first full-length ballet in over one hundred years.

The door opened and the man was sitting in a chair, as if he was waiting for her.

"Innichka, I have a present for you. For the production of *The Nutcracker*."

He handed her a pair of beautiful satin pink pointe shoes,

53

adorned with Swarovski crystals. Inna had never seen anything so beautiful. She pushed her long blonde hair out of her face to get a better look. "These are gorgeous. But I can never repay you for them. My family barely scrapes by as it is."

He clasped his hands over his face. His dark hair had a few streaks of gray and there were tiny lines around his deep blue eyes. "You don't owe me anything, Inna. I've watched you dance. You remind me of two ballerinas that I once danced with. You move like them. One day, you will make a beautiful Snow Queen."

The snow queen! That was Inna's favorite role! Before this man had moved here, Inna dreamed of dancing the role ever since she saw a production of the Bolshoi Ballet's *Nutcracker* on television. But with the closest ballet school fifty miles away, there was little hope of that ever happening. "It's my dream to be a ballerina. I will work so hard—I won't ever let you down. You're the best thing that ever happened to our town."

He smiled and turned away from her. His eyes seemed to be staring off into the distance. She followed his gaze and realized that he was fixated on a small snow globe. It had a beautiful ballerina and her king, twirling inside, dancing to "The Waltz of the Snowflakes."

About the Author

ALANA ALBERTSON IS the former President of RWA's Chick Lit and Young Adult chapters. She holds a Masters of Education from Harvard and a Bachelor of Arts in English from Stanford. A recovering professional ballroom dancer, Alana currently writes contemporary romance. She lives in San Diego, California, with her husband, two sons, and four dogs. When she's not spending her time needlepointing, dancing, or saving dogs from high kill shelters through Pugs N Roses, the rescue she founded, she can be found watching episodes of Homeland, or Dallas Cowboys Cheerleaders: Making the Team. Please visit her website at www.alanaalbertson.com.

ALSO AVAILABLE BY AUTHOR

LOVE WALTZES IN
WALTZ ON THE WILD SIDE
INVINCIBLE
CONCEIT